All children have a strong desire to read to themselves...

and a sense of achievement when they can do so. The **read it yourself** series has been devised to satisfy their desire, and to give them that sense of achievement. The series is graded for specific reading ages, using simple vocabulary and sentence structure, and the illustrations complement the text so that the words and pictures together form an integrated whole.

LADYBIRD BOOKS, INC.
Lewiston, Maine 04240 U.S.A.
© LADYBIRD BOOKS LTD MCMLXXVIII
Loughborough, Leicestershire, England

Printed in England

Peter and the Wolf

by Fran Hunia
illustrated by Kathie Layfield

Ladybird Books

Peter is at home.

He wants to go and play
in the meadow,
but the gate is closed.

A bird is up in a tree
in the meadow.

The bird sings to Peter,
''Come on, Peter.
Come into the meadow.''

"Yes," says Peter.

"Here I come."

He opens the gate
and goes into the meadow.

Peter plays in the meadow.

The bird sings
up in the tree.

A duck comes
into the meadow.

She goes for a swim
in the pond.

The bird flies down
from the tree.

He says to the duck,
"You are a silly bird.
You can't fly.
See, I can fly."

The duck says to the bird,
"*You* are a silly bird.
You can't swim.
See, I can swim."

They argue and argue.

A cat comes up
to the pond.

He sees the duck
and the bird.
''I want that bird,''
he says.

The duck and the bird
argue and argue.

They don't see the cat.

The cat gets closer
to the duck and the bird.

Peter sees the cat.

"Look out!" he says.

The bird flies up
into the tree.

The duck swims away.

They are safe.

The cat looks up at the bird.

Out comes Peter's
grandfather.

"Come here, Peter,"
he calls.

"Come home with me.
It is not safe out here
in the meadow.
A wolf may come
and get you."

Grandfather takes Peter
out of the meadow.

They go home,
and Grandfather closes
the gate.

A wolf comes out
into the meadow.

He sees the cat, the duck,
and the bird.

The cat sees the wolf
and jumps up
into the tree,
with the bird.

They are safe.

The duck sees the wolf.

She jumps out of the water
and runs away.

The wolf runs after the duck.

The wolf gets the duck
and swallows her down
in one gulp.

The cat and the bird
are up in the tree.

They are safe.

The wolf goes
around and around the tree,
but he can't get up.

Peter looks out
into the meadow
and sees the wolf.

He goes inside
to get a rope.

Peter takes the rope
up into the tree.

He is going
to get the wolf.

Peter says to the bird,
"Fly around the wolf,
please.
I want to get him
with this rope."

The bird flies down.

The bird flies
around and around the wolf.

Peter ties the rope
to the tree.

He lets the rope down.

Peter gets the wolf.

The wolf jumps up and down.

He can't get away.

Some hunters come.

They are looking
for the wolf.

"Look," says Peter.
"Here is the wolf.
He can't get away.
Please help me
take him
to the zoo."

They all go to the zoo.

Peter and the bird...
the hunters with the wolf...
Grandfather...
and the cat.